THE RETURN OF
THE SMURFETTE

Peyo

THE RETURN OF THE SMURFETTE

A **SMURFS** GRAPHIC NOVEL BY *Peyo*

PAPERCUTZ™
NEW YORK

SMURFS GRAPHIC NOVELS AVAILABLE FROM PAPERCUTZ ™

COMING SOON:

THE SMURFS graphic novels are available in paperback for $5.99 each and in hardcover for $10.99 each at booksellers everywhere. You can also order online at www.papercutz.com. Or call 1-800-886-1223, Monday through Friday, 9 – 5 EST. MC, Visa, and AmEx accepted. To order by mail, please add $4.00 for postage and handling for first book ordered, $1.00 for each additional book and make check payable to NBM Publishing. Send to: Papercutz, 160 Broadway, Suite 700, East Wing, New York, NY 10038.

THE SMURFS graphic novels are also available digitally wherever e-books are sold.

PAPERCUTZ.COM

THE RETURN OF THE SMURFETTE ♥

SMURF™ © Peyo - 2012 - Licensed through Lafig Belgium - www.smurf.com

English translation copyright © 2012 by Papercutz.
All rights reserved.

"Romeos and Smurfette"
BY YVAN DELPORTE AND PEYO

"The Return of the Smurfette"
BY YVAN DELPORTE AND PEYO

"The Smurf Garden"
BY PEYO

"The Handy Smurf"
BY PEYO

"Halloween"
BY PEYO

"Smurferies"
BY PEYO

Joe Johnson, SMURFLATIONS
Adam Grano, SMURFIC DESIGN
Janice Chiang, LETTERING SMURFETTE
Matt. Murray, SMURF CONSULTANT
Beth Scorzato, SMURF COORDINATOR
Michael Petranek, ASSOCIATE SMURF
Jim Salicrup, SMURF-IN-CHIEF

PAPERBACK EDITION ISBN: 978-1-59707-292-2
HARDCOVER EDITION ISBN: 978-1-59707-293-9

PRINTED IN THE US JULY 2013 BY LIFETOUCH PRINTING
5126 FOREST HILLS CT
LOVES PARK, IL 61111

Papercutz books may be purchased for business or promotional use. For information on bulk purchases please contact Macmillan Corporate and Premium Sales Department at (800) 221-7945 x5442.

DISTRIBUTED BY MACMILLAN
FOURTH PAPERCUTZ PRINTING

ROMEOS AND SMURFETTE

A hundred Smurfs were living in peace.
A Smurfette came along
But that's another story.[1]

You were wondering what became of her.
She's doing well.
From time to time, she comes back to the village, and
As these stories will show, she hasn't changed.

Peyo *Y. Delporte

[1] A story told in SMURFS #4 "The Smurfette."

What's smurfing on? Could it, by any chance...

Oh, yes! It's spring!

Blamed millions of billions of smurfs!

Something bothering you, Farmer Smurf?

Well, it's 'cause of those durned birds... a-eating all my good grain...

Why don't you make a good scarecrow?

Scarecrow? Hmmm... a scarecrow! I'd need some clothes... I don't have any!

Ask Vanity Smurf... he'll certainly smurf you a favor.

Good idea, Papa Smurf, and I'll head right over!

Hey, Vanity Smurf, I was wondering if you'd help me dress up a scarecrow...

I'd love to!

In fact, I have here a few WONderful pieces... this veil of raw silk... a yard of lamé brocade... And also this braid of Alençon lace...

The obvious stitching will smurf a crazy style on the appliqué!

TIKKATATIKKATA

With a naughty, little trifle on the hat, it will be fiercely smurf!

Later...

Well, Farmer Smurf? Happy with the new scarecrow?

Blamed Vanity Smurf! I don't want to talk about it... it's so well smurfed birds from sixty miles around come to admire it!

7

All right! Shoo! Get! Smurf away!

Go away, you smurficy!

Well, Farmer Smurf? More problems with the birds?

Yes, Papa Smurf! And that there scarecrow's way too purty to scare 'em!

What if you asked Architect Smurf for a statue...?

So, you got it? I'm needing something that looks real!

Understood!

Let's see... whom could I smurf as a model? Hefty Smurf? Brainy Smurf?

No, I have a better idea!

There! Now I just have to smurf it to Farmer Smurf's field!

Heh heh! Wasn't my idea good? I don't see any more birds!

Sure, the statue is great for not having any more birds, but...

I wonder if the scarecrow wasn't better!

48

She loves me a little, a lot...

...smurfily, passionately, madly...

...not!

That wasn't a good one! I'm going to smurf another one!

She loves me a little, a lot, smurfily, passionately, madly...

..NOT!

It's not possible!...'loves... 'little... 'lot.. 'ily... 'nately... 'madly... NOT!

⸲Grrumbleble!⸴ NOT! NOT! ✷⚡✦⬡... NOT! NOT!

She really doesn't smurf me at all! ⸲Sniff!⸴

Hee hee hee! And I left only seven petals on each daisy! Hee hee hee!

!

Peyo 12

Ah! I'm going to smurf an everlasting monument destined for future generations who will smurf the message of my great affection upon it! To work!

TAP
TAP
TAP

For Smurf's sake, this rock is smurfily hard!

NOK NOK NOK

And this hammer and chisel are smurfily heavy!

≒Phew!≒ I'm smurfed out!

I'm going to continue with a brush instead!

Oh, drat!

Out of paint! All the same, I'm not going to go all the way back to the village just to smurf back!

Hey, you wouldn't have a piece of chalk?

?

THE RETURN OF THE SMURFETTE

Life is calm and peaceful here. We are, it's true, in the village of the Smurfs...

Yum yum! Who's going to be smurfing this nice cake?

I-- !?

⊙✱✦!Ƨ⊚☀ Who's the smurf who smurfed on my cake?

There! It's a bird! He's carrying a piece of paper in his smurf!

Look what you've smurfed! Aren't you ashamed?

Hey! Smurfette wrote this! We have to go tell Papa Smurf quickly.

PAPA SMURF! PAPA SMURF! IT'S A LETTER FROM SMURFETTE!

Me, I don't like letters!

My dear little Smurfs, I have something very, very smurf to smurf you. I'll come visit tomorrow, Smurfette.

It's her!

She's coming!

Quick! My most ensmurfing scent.

FWISSHH
FWISSSH

I'm going to smurf her a magnificent present!

She loves smurf tart with smurfed cream!

I'll have to resmurf my "Serenade to the Smurfette"!

You, o you, my Smurfette what rhymes with Smurfette?

Ah dear me, I can sense I'll be dreaming about Smurfette!

That night...

Pellet, marionette, barrette...

...and stick it in the oven!

Toot! PWAAA!

ZZZ

And the next day...

Don't smurf! I was here first!

Who? You? Yes, my smurf! I was!

THERE SHE IS!

Yoohoo! Hello, hello!

You haven't smurfed! You're as beasmurfiful as ever!

The most beasmurfiful! The most ensmurfing!

Hey! I have some flowers for you!

My compliments, my dear little Smurfette! To what do we owe the honor...?

Well, I've smurfed a great decision! I'm going to get married to one of you!

WITH ME?

No! With ME!

No way! ME!

ME! ME!

Of course, I'm the one you'll smurf! That way, you'll be Mama Smurfette!

No, but just smurf at that old Smurf! Ha ha ha!

Still wanting to smurf the Smurfette! At his age!

It's smurf and it's no longer smurf!

IT'S ME! IT'S ME! IT'S ME!

If you dare smurf her, I'll smurf my smurf on your smurf!

I'M THE ONE she'll smurf!

Come now! Calm down! Listen closely! I'll marry the first Smurf who brings me THE MOON!

And that night, when the moon rose in the sky...

The moon is low! Now's the time! I'm going to smurf it for you like a flower!

DRAT! A little too short!

Why... there it is! That's it!

YIPPEE! I smurfed it! I'm Smurfette's future smurf!

There! It's smurfed in the pond!

HUP!

Well? What smurfed to it? It smurfed through the strings of my net!?

Into the moon! My arrow never misses its smurf!

TWIPP

3

THE SMURF GARDEN

Brrr...
it's cold!

Look! Why it's full of little bugs!

My cake!

What a nice picnic!

Me, I don't like little bugs!

We absolutely must fix this place up! Come on! Let's resmurf to the village!

Hello, Handy Smurf! We need you and... uh... your tools!

Yeah! Like usual, eh? Sure! Go in and smurf whatever you need!

Can I borrow this hammer?

Ah?

Come on, Dopey Smurf, those are pliers!

You haven't seen the bottle-smurfener?

Where are the screws?

You mean: the smurf-opener?

BAMB CLANG BAM BANG GYZZZZ BONG POP TAP

And there! Smurf my folding chair! I'll open it...

I'll unfold...

I 🌀★💥🔧

WAAAH!

Watch out! Let me through!

Peyo

2

So, Lazy Smurf, that porch swing?

I'm thinking about it! I can't stop thinking about it!

Hey! Come look at my barbesmurf that's burns with no smoke!

BOOOM

This thing's not very practical for cutting the grass! There must be some way to improve upon it!

If I smurf a smurf-throttle here, which links to a rotor whose reduction system produces the desired power...

BANG BAN BANG

And voila! Let's see how it smurfs!

⇗Whew!⇖ It's heavy... and tiring!

ACHITTYITTYTACHITTY

If I remove the reduction smurf, take out the rotor, and cut the smurf-throttle...

I get this lighter, less bulky model! I'm a GENIUS!

And me! Look what I smurfed!

Well, Dopey Smurf, what are you going to do with that big rake?

Well, smurf up the really big leaves, say!

Dopey Smurf is crazy!

All right! It's late! Let's get to bed! We'll continue tomorrow!

That night, on the other side of the forest...

Come, Azrael, we're going to look for some poisonous mushrooms!

Meow!

I'd so like to catch a Smurf one day! Only one! Just a little one!

♪♫

Why... it looks like the Smurfs came here! They even had a picnic!

Heh heh! That gives me an idea!

I'VE GOT THEM!!

Quick, Azrael! Let's go back!

To work!

?

HA! HA! HA!

BLINK BAM BING BANG

And the next day...

Hello, Smurfette! Where are you going?

I'm going to pick some strawberries!

TRALALA-LALA

?!

20

HEY! SMURFS! COME AND HAVE A LOOK!

What is it? What's going on?

Look at this sign! That must be smurfily nice! What if we went?

COME ONE COME SMURF The Garden of Delights Is this way

Uh... is that very safe?

Why? Are you afraid?

Afraid?

US?

Who?

Ha! Ha!

Let's go then!

You smurf ahead of me!

Me? Why me?

The Garden of Delights

Oh! It's so pretty!

A swing!

Games!

Don't go in there! It's a trap!

A pool!

Me, I don't like traps!

Who could have smurfed all this?

I don't know! Anyway, it's smurfily well smurfed!

Is it nice?

Excellent!

Ha! Ha! Ha!

Let's go!

CREE

HEY!?

SNAPP

And now the tear gas! Ha ha ha!

SWUNK

Oww! My eyes! It stings! I can't smurf anything!

COFF COFF!

SPROINK

?

?

?

Hup!

SPROING

But... where's the water?

It went out that hole! There's no way to smurf out of here!

What... what's happening?

NOIIING

HELP! SOMEONE SMURFED GLUE ON THE SWING!

GARGAMEL!

A trap! It was a trap!

Quick! I have to tell Papa Smurf!

Hahaaa! I've got you little monsters this time!

Little monsters? No way, haven't you ever smurfed at yourself, you old goat?

I warned them, but they didn't smurf to me! And now they're all prisoners...

Arm yourselves! We have to smurf them!

BAWHHATTAAAA

CHARGE!

No, Dopey Smurf, that's not a weapon, that's a RAKE!

Oh?

There he is! ATTACK!

RELEASE YOUR PRISONERS, GARGAMEL!

The Smurfs!

Papa Smurf! We're saved!

END

THE HANDY SMURF

Do you know the Smurfs are happy, little beings? They love using trowels and hammers. Oh, yes! There's a handyman lurking inside of every Smurf!

While Lazy Smurf made a silent alarm clock...

Jokey Smurf makes presents that explode...

Tailor Smurf uses his sewing machine...

Well, what? This is a sewing machine, isn't it?

Harmony Smurf tinkers with his instruments, but with no results. He keeps playing out of tune!

And when Painter Smurf wants to hang his paintings...

BAM BAM BAM

BAM OWWWWW

...he calls on Nurse Smurf!

@!?★#

In short, all the Smurfs—

No! Me, I don't like tinkering!

26

That day...

Papa Smurf will be celebrating his 542nd birthday! We have to smurf him a present!

Yes! But what?

We could smurf him a makeover!

A cane?

Crutches!

Or a bib!

Hee hee hee!

♪Ahem!♪

?

Oh, smurf! Papa Smurf!

Some dumbbells?

A racing hat?

Some raspberry liqueur?

We'll have to smurf something "young" for him.

Yes!

What if we smurfed him a big, giant cake?

Hey, that's a smurftastic idea!

Me, I don't like ideas!

Let's go to Baker Smurf's!

Sorry, it's impossible! Yesterday, I tried a new recipe for smurf baba and today I'm soooo sick!

Maybe I can help you?

Oh! Smurfette! You'd do that?

You're too kind!

Your cake will be way better than Baker Smurf's!

What kind of cake are you going to smurf for us, Smurfette?

A caramel cream smurf?

A smurf baba?

Some smurf fritters?

No, no! A layer cake! I have the recipe here!

I need some flour, milk, butter, whipped egg whites...

...fresh cream, sugar syrup, honey...

...three shoe nails...

What do you mean three shoe nails?!?

JOKEY SMURF! COME HERE!

HEE HEE HEE!

HEE HEE HEE!

HEE HEE!

AND ALL OF YOU, OUT! I DON'T WANT ANYONE UNDERFOOT!

Okay! And now to work!

Oh! This spoon is twisted!

I'll go ask Handy Smurf to fix it for me!

Yoohoo! Handy Smurf! I have a small favor to ask of you!

NOK NOK NOK

I DON'T HAVE TIME!

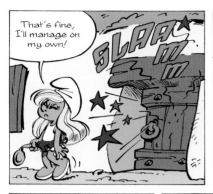

That's fine, I'll manage on my own!

SLAAM

There's just no way to make a decent hole! I've tried everything: the chisel, the hammer, the sickle, the hot iron...

Nothing works! I get ovals, squares, wonky holes... when the wood doesn't break!

I have to smurf up some other means for doing them! Let's see! If the sliding gear on the calibresmurf of the F pulley and the driving power is...

EUREKA!

It's got to smurf! Must get to it!

All night long...

CLANG BANG POW DZOOIING OW!

So there! I'll fill the machine body with honey...

Which will attract bees who, out of happiness, will beat their wings!

BZZZZZZZZ

The wind they make will power the helices attached to a shaft upon which I'll smurf a drill bit! I close the box! I hit the release and...

DZZIIII

IT WORKS! IT WORKS!

Peyo

4

30

Smurfette! Smurfette! Look what I smurfed!

I DON'T HAVE TIME!

Who's coming to smurf strawberries with me? ♪

Me!

Me!

Me!

Me, I don't like me's!

She's right! I wasn't very smurf to her! I'll have to smurf something to be smurfgiven.

What if I... Yes! That's a great idea!

Yoohoo! Anyone in here?

No! There's nobody!

Let's go!

DZIII

There! I'm sure she'll be happy!

Since you're being so nice, you can help me make the cake!

Really?

Cool!

Thanks, Smurfette!

Here's some wood for the fire!

Careful with the fruit!

Hmmm! It's good!

Who wants to whip my egg whites?

NO, ME!

ME!

Okay! Now we just have to put the batter in the cake pan and smurf everything into the oven!

THE END

More ROMEOS AND SMURFETTE

Yes, Papa Smurf, I think I'm going to marry one of you! But I don't yet know which one!

ME, SMURFETTE!

NO! ME!

ME!

Come now, there's no reason to hesitate! I'm no youngster, but I'm still very spry, despite my gray hairs! And then you'd become Mama Smurfette!

Well, uh...

I'll smurf you music all day long! I'll even smurf you some at night!

I'll smurf you big, fat cakes, smurf-babas, smurf-fritters, with lots of smurfed cream...

I'll smurf verses to you, o Smurfette!

Uh, me, salads, turnips, for smurf's sake!

I'll smurf beautiful dresses for you!

I'll tinker together lots of contraptions for you!

You can smurf on my strength to defend you!

I'm the one you should smurf, for my smurf is sighing and, as the proverb says: the smurf that sighs doesn't have what it desires, I'll tell Papa Smurf, who...

I don't know what I'll smurf for you, but I'll smurf it!

Me, I don't want to get married!

He's the one I want to marry!

! !?

Peyo 30

Uh, say, Smurfette, am I the one you wanted to smurf in wedded bliss?

Or me?

Or me? You have to decide!

Me!

Yes! Which one of us are you marrying?

I smurfily don't know! You're all so nice!

Yes, but I'm nicer than the others!

That's not true, I am!

I'd smurf anything for you!

Anything at all? Is that true? You'll smurf me my breakfast in bed every morning?

And you'll smurf the dishes every day? And the clothes-smurfing every week?

You'll also have to do the ironing, that you help me fold the sheets, smurf the dust on the furniture, smurf the rugs...

Untangle the wool, do the deep cleaning, smurf the potatoes, dig out the garden, cut the wood, make the beds, shine my shoes, do the mopping, smurf the brass and silver, and also...

But... but where did they all go?

Peyo

31

HALLOWEEN

Apples? At this time of the year?

It's a magic apple tree, smurfed by the witch of the forest! It smurfs fruit all year long!

A witch?!

Maybe they're poisonous apples!

No, you chicken! I've already smurfed some. They're really good!

He's right! It's full of red apples!

Careful! Smurf into the bushes! The witch is coming out of her home!

I'm going to find some toads to brew my potions! ⸱Nyak nyak!⸱

Yum, ⸱crunch!⸱ Mmm! It's very good!

OH! LOOK OUT! The witch is already coming back this way!

I'll get you, you little thieves!

She's seen us!

Let's smurf out of here!

You little apple snatchers! I'm gonna catch you, you harmful, wretched gnomes!

You won't escape my wicked powers! I'll cast a spell on you, you cursed blue dwarves! Be transformed into pumpkins! Abracadabra! Abracadabra!

© Peyo

:Whew!: We lost her! Quick, let's smurf to the village!

Hee hee! She's just a part-time witch! Her spell didn't smurf!

WATCH OUT!

CRASH

EEEEEEE!

For smurf's sake! All my pumpkins!

Don't get mad! We'll help you smurf them back!

?

Your pumpkins are nice! Can we smurf four of them?

And do what with 'em?

:PHEW:

To disguise ourselves and play tricks in the village! Today is *Halloween!*

Well, yes then! We have to smurf traditions!

A little later...

Hey, look, the little Smurfs are in costumes!

We're ghosts!

Trick or treat!

BOOO!

GRR!

Ha! Ha! Whoo-hoo! Take the confetti, it's for you!

When I was a youngster, we'd smurf into the village shouting:"Smurf us some treats or we'll smurf you some tricks!" Ah, those were the good old days!

Thanks, Papa Smurf!

Let's go see Smurfette! We'll try it out on her!

It'll be funny!

Hee hee hee!

Trick or treat?

Neither! Get going, I have work to do!

Too bad, you asked for it! Hee hee!

Stop! You'll make a mess everywhere! I'll smurf you some cakes!

© Peyo

2

It worked! Let's go see Grouchy Smurf!

Trick or treat?

Me, I hate tricks! I like treats and I hate pumpkins!

It's just for laughs!

I hate laughing!

Bah! He's no fun! Let's go to Jokey Smurf's!

Trick or treat, Jokey Smurf?

Hey, here are some surprise treats!

Surprise treats! What are they?

BOOM

Well, as surprises go...

Ha ha ha! I got you! I sure got you!

Let's go see Greedy Smurf!

Oh yeah! Heh heh!

Ah, this is for Halloween! Come in, come in, I've been expecting you!

Oh yeah?

Dig in! I smurfed you a few sweets! Some buns, some chocolate mousse, some raspberry smurfs, and also...

WOW!

© Peyo

A little later...

My stomach hurts!! Ohhh!

I ate too much! ⸫Hiccup!⸫

Wait! There's still some cherry pie left and some smurf cobbler!

3

40

We're the little Smurfs upon whom you cast a spell! You remember turning us into pumpkins!

We've come back to haunt you!

By the infernal flames, that's the first time I've managed to cast a spell and have it work! It's frightening!

BOOOOOOOOO

Now's our chance!

HUP! I smurf the candle!

I got the candle! Get ready for the next part!

Hee hee hee!

I don't trust those pumpkins! Quick, my witch's broomstick!

!?! No light?! Where's the candle?

AHHHHH!!!

Now's the time! It's my turn to smurf! Hee hee hee!

AHHHHH! Yet another head!!

BOOOOOO!

Be gone, cursed ghosts!!

SLAM

© Peyo

BONK
OWW

Come on, Papilio, let's run! Hee hee hee!

I had nothing to do with it! Look... a Smurf! He's running away! He's the guilty one!

Ah, the little trickster! He surely didn't come alone!

I don't see anything! I'll never catch them!

On such a dark night, only a Jack-o'-Lantern could find them with his magic lantern!

Jack! Of course! Let's call for him!

Jack-o'-Lantern... Jack-o'-Lantern... come and help us! Come!

POOOF

Me!

Here I am! Who called for me?

No, me!

@※!☠* Help us catch those Smurfs who are hiding in those bushes!

That way!

Wait! I must explain something to you!

I carry off into the darkness whoever utters my name on the night of Halloween! So? Which of the two of you called for me?

It wasn't me!

It was him!

Are you mocking me?!

You don't play around with Jack-o'-Lantern! You'll both be punished!

BONK

POOOF

And here's your punishment, old fool!

Uh, oh! My nose! He's transformed my lovely nose into sausages!

HA HA HA!

You think that's funny?!

Farewell! And remember your lesson! Ha ha ha!

It's all your fault, you good for nothing sorcerer! !#*

OWW OWWIE! OUCH!

BAM BAM BAM

HA HA HA!

Hee hee hee!

Later...

Where did you go? We're smurfing for you for the big Halloween party!

Yippee! We're coming!

BOO OOO BOOOOO OOOOOO

YIPPEE

BOO OOO

YIPPEE

GRRR

BOO OOO

GRRR

BOO OOO

OOOOO

BOO OOO

Meanwhile...

I'll get my revenge! I'll get my revenge!

© Peyo

THE END

Welcome to the tear-jerking tenth SMURFS graphic novel by Peyo from Papercutz, the poetic and passionate publishers of great graphic novels for all ages. I'm Jim Salicrup, your hopelessly romantic Smurf-in-Chief. Ever since THE SMURFS #4 "The Smurfette" was published we've been bombarded with requests and outright demands for the return of the Smurfette! Even the Smurfs themselves were eager for her to return to the Smurf Village! Well, the long wait is over! The Smurfette's back, in all her smurfy glory! And we're not just talking about her starring role in the The Smurfs DVD, which features the Smurfs in their big-screen 3-D blockbuster! She's back in our pages where she belongs!

As you can see for yourself, where the Smurfette goes, trouble follows! That's why she left the Smurfs Village the first time. This time around she hasn't changed much—all she's asking for is the moon! (See what she missed by not being around during THE SMURFS #7 "The Astrosmurf"?) It also looks like she'll be sticking around a lot longer! In fact, she plays a very important role in THE SMURFS #11 "The Smurf Olympics," coming soon to booksellers everywhere.

And speaking of the lovable Smurfette, we should mention that like several other Papercutz graphic novel series, THE SMURFS were originally published in French—the language of love. Providing "smurflations" is none other than E. Joe Johnson. He is a Professor of French and Spanish and the chair of the Department of Humanities at

Smurflator E. Joe Johnson

Clayton State University in Metro Atlanta, Georgia. Pretty impressive, eh? He specializes in 18th-century French studies and has published five books, multiple scholarly articles, and scores of translations of French graphic novels for NBM Publishing and Papercutz. He thinks that working on THE SMURFS is pretty smurftastic.

We couldn't agree more with the good professor! We'd love to talk more about the Smurfs, but we're late for our appointment with our personal trainer! We're trying to get in shape for the Smurf Olympics! Smurf you later!

Smurf, always smurf.
Practice makes smurf.
For it's at the foot of the smurf that one smurfs
the least.
Yes!

Everything smurfs to he who smurfs.

SMURFERIES

THERE ARE NONE SO SMURF AS THOSE WHO WILL NOT SMURF

Hey! Smurfs, come help me smurf this bag of flour!

Hey! Yo! Did you hear me?

Now what? Have they gone deaf?

Well done!

Okay, I'll smurf it all by myself! But one of you should go smurf me some sarsaparilla! Do you hear? Hey! Do you hear?

Your turn!

What's going on? This sudden deafness isn't normal!

Cheater!

I need some wood for the fire!

WOOD FOR THE FIRE!

Nothing works. They're as deaf as a doorsmurf!

Darn, missed!

I wonder if there's any way to cure this illness?

Yoohoo, this big sarsaparilla cake I just made for my little Smurfs looks really good...

A CAKE! AND A SARSAPARILLA ONE!

CRUNCH

YUM

GNAP

My word! They're cured!

HOISTED ON HIS OWN SMURF

Look, Papa Smurf, a thief has smurfed another of my cakes this morning!

Trust me! I'll smurf the guilty party!

Thanks, Papa Smurf!

You two, what did you smurf this morning?

I smurfed ball with him!

And me with him!

Papa Smurf, I was smurfing good advice to Grumpy Smurf, because we must listen to the wisdom of our elders and--

Me, I don't like ands!

Me, of course, I was smurfing in my field, while listening to Poet Smurf!

I was smurfing, if you please, with Farmer Smurf.

Me, too!

I smurfed late in bed!

I practiced my scales!

I stuck my fingers in my ears!

I caught a cold!

I crocheted a lovely, little cotton cap!

Hmm... let's proceed by eliminasmurf!

So, Papa Smurf, did you smurf the guilty party?

Yes!

ONLY ONE has no alibi. **HE**, therefore, is the one who did it!

Who's that?

...Me!

49

> Pfff!

> I am smurfed up with this, I am so so smurfed up with this!

> YAWN!

> ?

> AH?

> All right! Smurf out of here, you lucky smurf!

> REALLY?... FINALLY!!

> We really should ask Architect Smurf to smurf us some small figurines for our chess matches.

> Want to cheat?

> Are you crazy?

> Yes!

> ...And I told him that's no reason to smurf to me like that...

> CHECK-SMURF!

> I'M DONE! I'M ALL DONE! TRALALA!

> Why are you smurfing me to be careful and not let myself be captured?

50

DO NOT SMURF THE SMURF'S NAME IN VAIN...

Well? Well? What's that I'm hearing there?

It's this smurfing mallet that smurfed on my foot, Papa Smurf!

That's no reason for smurfing curse words! Go smurf your mouth out with a brush and soap! Go on! Get a smurf on!

All right! And don't ever smurf curse words again! Is that undersmurfed?

Undersmurfed, Papa Smurf!

THERE'S NO SMURFCOUNTING FOR TASTE

GNAP! GNAP!

A PURPLE SMURF! [1]

GNAP! GNAP!

RUN FOR YOUR SMURFS!

He's going to bite us!

And we'll all turn purple!

Smurf yourselves!

GNAP! GNAP! GNAP!

NO! NO! NO!

Quick! We have to smurf some tuberose pollen, because Papa Smurf always says that smurfing some tuberose pollen on a purple Smurf will turn him back...

⸗Flebelebeleb!⸗

Hee hee hee! I really got them!

Now I'm going to smurf a nice bath and...

Who smurfed my purple paint? That one's indelible and won't ever come off!

(1) See THE SMURFS #1 "The Purple Smurfs"

Hey? What's that smurf there?

It's a smurf!

Oh? What's a smurf for?

Well, for smurfing!

For smurfing what?

Some smurf with smurf!

Really? And how does it smurf?

It's simple! You smurf on this smurf, and the smurf smurfs into smurf!

And if you smurf on this other smurf, do you smurf some smurfed smurfs?

Ah, no!

Why?

Because the smurf is smurfed for smurfing smurf with smurf and not smurfed smurfs.

Ah?

But if you smurfed on the two smurfs at the same time?

Don't ever smurf that, you'd smurf the whole thing!

Smurf closely to me, I'm going to smurf you how this smurf smurfs! You see this smurf here?

Yes!

Okay! Well, when you smurf on this smurf, you're smurfing a series of smurfed intersmurfed between them, which, by desmurfing, smurf by the smurf some smurf to smurf! Do you smurf?

Yes, yes!

He doesn't seem like he undersmurfed! But that was clear, wasn't it?.

86

Peyo

DRESSING FOR SMURFCESS

Did you see?

Oh! Nice!

TONIGHT
GRAND COSTUME PARTY
★ WITH MANY PRIZES.

What are you going to smurf up as?

Ah! I'm not telling! You'll smurf it tonight!

Heh heh! I think that was a good idea that I smurfed up with. In fact, I'll have to smurf myself up, too!

Let's see, let's see. Ah! That's it! I smurfed it!

It'll be the most original disguise!

Why didn't you disguise yourself?

But I **AM** disguised! I'm Papa Smurf!!

3 1901 05845 6940